Dear Parent:

You are about to read a brand new version of a familiar folk tale. Joanna Cole's sprightly adaptation coupled with popular children's book illustrator Kate Duke's bright and colorful illustrations breathe new life into this old tale.

Folk tales are a wonderful addition to a children's home library. They are the kind of stories that you remember forever. Whether it's "Little Red Riding Hood" or "Three Billy Goats Gruff," these stories have been enjoyed for generations by people in all cultures. Did you know, for example, that there are seven hundred different versions of Cinderella, including one in Chinese?

This is a book which can be shared with the whole family. It may spark interest in other folk tales. You can find collections of stories or individual retellings in your local library. We hope you will find more and more stories from the Weekly Reader Book Club that are worth reading and remembering.

Sincerely,

Stephen Fraser

Stephen Fraser
Senior Editor
Weeky Reader Book Club

Weekly Reader Children's Book Club Presents

It's Too Noisy!

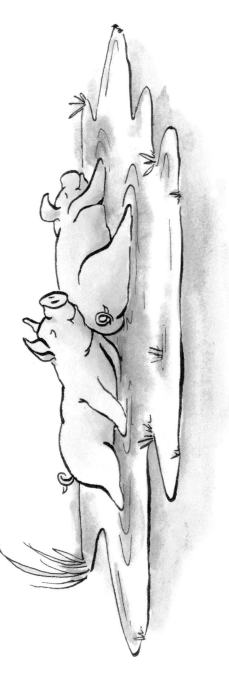

by Joanna Cole

illustrated by Kate Duke

Thomas Y. Crowell   New York

This book is a presentation of Newfield Publications, Inc.
Newfield Publications offers book clubs for children
from preschool through high school. For further
information write to: **Newfield Publications, Inc.,**
4343 Equity Drive, Columbus, Ohio 43228.

Published by arrangement with Thomas Y. Crowell,
a division of HarperCollins Publishers, Inc.
Newfield Publications is a federally registered trademark
of Newfield Publications, Inc.
Weekly Reader is a federally registered trademark
of Weekly Reader Corporation.

IT'S TOO NOISY!

Text copyright © 1989 by Joanna Cole
Illustrations copyright © 1989 by Kate Duke
Printed in the U.S.A. All rights reserved.
1 2 3 4 5 6 7 8 9 10
First Edition

Library of Congress Cataloging-in-Publication Data
Cole, Joanna
It's too noisy!

Summary: Unable to stand his noisy and overcrowded
home any longer, a farmer goes to the Wise Man for
advice.
[1. Folklore, Jewish] I. Duke, Kate, ill.
II. Title.
PZ8.1.C668It 1989   [398.2][E]   88-3865
ISBN 0-690-04735-5
ISBN 0-690-04737-1 (lib. bdg.)

To my great-nephews
Bartley
Christopher
Michael
—J.C.

To my mother
—K.D.

Once there was a little house. Do you know who lived there?

A poor farmer lived in that little house with his wife,

a grandmother, a grandfather,

lots of children,

and a little bitty baby in a crib!

Day and night
there was always
a lot of
yelling,
singing,
snoring,
laughing,
fighting,
and crying.
It was too noisy!

The poor farmer wanted quiet!

He went to the Wise Man.

"Wise Man, Wise Man,"
he said.

"My house is full
of people.

It is too noisy!

Tell me what to do."

The Wise Man closed his eyes.
He thought and thought.
"Here is what to do," he said.
"Bring your rooster
and your chickens
into the house."

That is a funny thing to do,
thought the farmer.

But he did what
the Wise Man told him.
He got his rooster
and his chickens.
He put them in the house.

That night there
was a lot of
yelling,
singing,
snoring,
laughing,
fighting,
and crying.
And now there
was a lot of
clucking and crowing
too!

It was much too noisy!

The next day
the farmer went back
to the Wise Man.

"I put the rooster
and the chickens
in the house," he said.

"But it is worse than ever."

"Then you must put your pigs
and your sheep
in the house,"
said the Wise Man.

That is a *very* funny thing to do,
thought the farmer.

But he did what the Wise Man said.

That night
there was
yelling and singing,
snoring and laughing,
fighting and crying,
clucking and crowing.
And now there was
oinking and baaing too!

It was even worse than before!

The farmer went back
to the Wise Man.
"Noise! Noise! Noise!"
he said.
"I cannot stand it anymore!"
The Wise Man said,
"Now put your donkey
and your cow
in the house."

Is the Wise Man crazy?
thought the farmer.
But he did what
the Wise Man said.
He put his donkey
and his cow
in the house.

Now there was
yelling and singing,
snoring and laughing,
fighting and crying,
clucking and crowing,
oinking and baaing,
and braying and mooing.

It was so noisy the poor farmer did not sleep all night.

The farmer went back
to the Wise Man
one last time.

"Wise Man, Wise Man,
my house is like a barn!"
he cried.

"I cannot stand it."
The Wise Man smiled.

"Here is what to do," he said.

"Take all the animals
out of the house."
The farmer ran home.

He did just what the Wise Man said. He put out the chickens,

he put out the rooster,
he put out the pigs.
He put out the sheep
and the donkey
and the cow.

Was the little house still noisy? Well...

there was still
yelling and singing.
There was still
snoring and laughing.
There was even some
fighting and crying.
BUT...

there was

no clucking,

no crowing,

no oinking,

no baaing,

and—thank Heaven!—

there was no mooing

or braying either.

And to the farmer, that little house seemed as quiet as quiet can be.